BETWEEN THE LINES

BETWEEN THE LINES

Christopher Black
and
Matthew Bright

ROMAN *Books*
www.romanbooks.co.uk

British Library Cataloguing in Publication Data
A catalogue record for this book is available from the British Library.

Publisher: Suman Chakraborty

ROMAN Books
Kemp House, 152 City Road,
London EC1V 2NX, UK
2nd Floor, 38/3 Andul Road, Howrah 711109, WB, India
www.romanbooks.co.uk | www.romanbooks.co.uk

Printed and bound worldwide by
LSI and its partners

STRETTO

A FICTION SERIES

Series Editor: Jonathan Taylor

'... a plurality of independent and unmerged voices and consciousnesses.'

– Mikhail Bakhtin

Stretto is Italian for 'narrow' or 'close,' often used by musicians to refer to climactic sections of fugues where the voices overlap more closely, where the polyphonic texture is particularly intense. *Stretto* is now also a ground-breaking series of novels, novellas and short fictions, which takes on Mikhail Bakhtin's well-known conception of 'polyphonic' literature, intensifying it, playing with it, developing it in new contexts. Here are fictions which are multi-voiced, polyphonic, fugal in many different ways: fictions which are multi-perspectival; fictions which stage clashing, sometimes dissonant voices; fictions which hear from marginalised people; fictions which interweave human voices and musical voices; fictions which engage with voices from other places, other disciplines, other worlds. Above all, here are stories which are themselves musical, lyrical, dynamically contrapuntal.

Between the Lines is part of *Stretto* Fiction Series.

Christopher Black is a relentless optimist despite a hitherto total lack of success or recognition. He works as a Data Manager for clinical studies specialising in oncology and makes music with dated rock outfit Rhyn.

Matthew Bright is a writer, editor and designer who's never too sure what order those come in. He is the editor of several anthologies and his fiction had appeared in various places.

Matthew and Christopher studied writing together, where *Between the Lines* began.

BETWEEN THE LINES

CHRISTOPHER
BLACK

&

MATTHEW
BRIGHT

Two books are sitting   side by side

high on a *shelf*

in a room

(Whispering)

o   n   e

December 3rd 1882

M$_R$ D$_{ASHBY}$ W$_{ATCHED}$ the little coil of steam slowly rise from the cup of camomile and condense on the window pane before him. Resigned, he took a sip and stared out at the fields that lay beyond the manor house, blanketed in snow. He pondered wistfully how the weather might detrimentally affect the trade roads leading into town; travel often became troublesome during the festive season. Behind him, the ladies' voices wafted in from the drawing room.

"I was astounded to hear about the whole affair," one voice said.

"Oh, indeed," another replied. "It was a shock to us all. Especially considering Lady Farringdon's reputation. Never a hair out of place, such a fine example. One would never have supposed her to possess such a..."

"...*promiscuous* nature?" the first offered.

"..precisely! Promiscuous is the only word for it. But goodness, the mere association with a name of such repute seems unthinkable...mustn't she know her standing? Mind you, her recent suitors could scarcely be called the respectable type. All regular patrons of the local taverns, if you catch my meaning."

A knowing pause. "I imagine a person as free-willed as Lady Farringdon would be well aware of the reputation she carries—and jeopardises by the company she keeps."

A stifled giggle and topping up of glasses followed, and Mr Dashby allowed a deep sigh to escape him, fogging the pane inches away from his lips. Thus began the fourteenth Christmas he would spend at Compton House, with only the maids and butler for

Friday Night at Comptons, December 2006

Bex wiped Bacardi off her boobs, watched her fag-end burn out and stubbed it against the backed-up toilet. Tonight wasn't working—drilling bass-line, free drinks from sketchy blokes, teetering high heels and short skirt: none of it good.

A couple of years ago, when she was underage and used her cleavage as twin forms of ID to get past the bouncers on the door, she'd have been smashed out of her face and having a *Legendary* night, with a capital L. She wouldn't have been sneaking a fag in the toilets on her own either; she'd have been squashed in there with Lucy, necking pints nicked from oblivious drunks and screeching loudly about *that cute barman ohmigod he totally fancies you!*

She inhaled. *God, it's tragic to be a washed up club kid by eighteen.*

A burst of Nelly Furtado's *Promiscuous* was audible as the door swung open. A gaggle of girls stumbled in, vomiting gossip. "Oh my *god*, have you *seen* her? I know, right!"

Bex sucked up the last, glorious lungful.

"She is *such* a slut. Like, it's *so* inappropriate that she's dancing with *him*."

"I know! She totally asked me if it was okay, and I said, er… yeah, of course, like I care any more, but—*God*."

Bex swung the door open, popped her head through like a jack-in-the-box, and shrilled: "I know, *right!*"

The tarts were, predictably, applying more makeup, slathering black lines beneath their orangutan brows. One jumped, smearing mascara across her eyelid. Bex dropped the cigarette butt in the sink where it sizzled cathartically. Waving cheerily, she elbowed them aside.

company. Dashby was a respectable and amiable fellow, but notably for a man in his late twenties he bore the considerable lack of a personal life.

Of course, he had had several courting prospects before, but for all their infallible social graces, they rarely captured Dashby's interest for long. He had previously considered Lady Farringdon a potential, but when rumours of her indiscretions began to circulate, he became curiously intrigued. News of her late-night frivolities had granted her an air of decadence that Dashby found compelling. Ironic, then, that the very thing that excited him about Lady Farringdon should remove her from the list of appropriate inamoratas in the public eye. He finished the tea and set the cup emphatically on the table.

"All alone in here?" a voice from behind Dashby inquired. He turned to face a young, buxom girl in a red dress with auburn curls. She was smiling intently and cradling a glass of wine precariously in her left hand. "You must be the young Mr Dashby. Your father has been telling us all about you!"

Dashby bowed his head politely. "I sincerely hope not."

"What on earth are you doing in here on your own?" There was a slight slur to her words.

"Just taking a moment to myself."

The girl nodded and rolled her eyes as she advanced towards Dashby. "Well, you must come and join us, we're about to begin Charades! It's such a lark."

"That sounds... wonderful," he said, quite unable to think of anything that sounded worse. His attempt left her unconvinced.

"Oh, poppycock! You can be on my team!" She gave a slight curtsy, and smiled. "We haven't been introduced. I'm Samantha."

"William," Dashby said.

"What's your problem?"

Bex shrugged off the sideways looks, and strode out into the club with as much *cool-collected-ice-queen* as she could manage.

Then—*dammit*, did it have to be him?

There, dead centre of the lights, just as the music dropped to a thudding heartbeat bass, just as everyone became single frames of film jump-cutting in the flashing blue strobes, he looked straight up at her.

Breathe.

Sammy. *Sammy.* Exes went one of two ways: you broke up with them and then, when you saw them six months down the line, you either found every little thing about them annoying or you realised you were a complete idiot for letting them go, and that they were probably the love of your life.

No denying it, he did look unfairly attractive tonight.

I should go say hi.

That's a terrible idea.

No it's not.

Breathe.

She felt as if she was in slow motion as she moved through the jumping mass of people—the strobes lit him up in centimetre jumps. *See him, say hi, let him know you don't care, you don't need him—no, I can't—stop it, get it together, you broke up with him.*

He turned into her as she approached, and before she could speak, he grabbed her by the waist and kissed her. Fingers traced up the small of her back, slid under the edge of her top. His tongue parted her lips, thrust insistently against her own, and slid something small, hard and circular into her mouth.

"Well, William, won't you at least join me in a drink?"

He forced a smile. "That would be ecstasy."

"Glad to hear it!" she said, grabbing for his hand. "But later we must rejoin the others. Even strapping young men like you must face the music!"

As Samantha ushered Dashby along the hall towards the pantry, she cheerfully interrogated him over every detail concerning the manor and Dashby's life from birth to present day. She steered him with a hand on the small of his back as light as air, but Dashby felt its oppressive presence and braced himself for a long evening.

*　*　*

"THE WALTZ! OH, I do enjoy the waltz! Such a graceful dance, all that bending and lifting. A triumph of elegance, wouldn't you say?" She busied herself with a porcelain tea-set, her back turned to Dashby, who shifted uncomfortably by the door. "A wonderful display of dexterity!" she wittered digging into the sugar pot, "Of course, finding the right gentleman to waltz with, Mr Dashby, that's the real challenge. Would you like sugar?"

The question snapped Dashby out of a shallow daze. He released his firm grip on the door handle and accepted the cup of tea. With the accompanying silver spoon, he penetrated the surface of the hot liquid, and stirred fervently.

The ritual did much to relax him, and the soothing aroma of Earl Grey was carried up to him on a passage of steam. Samantha eyed him as he blew gently across the surface of the cup, making little tremors appear in the liquid as he slowly pulled it towards him.

Misjudging the force with which he tipped the cup, Dashby poured scalding fluid onto his chest. "Blast!" He dabbed the spot of

"Goddamit—Sammy! What was that?"

He grinned, far too wide. "You'll see."

She shoved him away. "I haven't done anything in ages."

Pulling her back: "Relax, sugar. Just ride the music."

Which, in retrospect, was when the night really kicked in. All of a sudden the bass was moving her feet, the chorus was in her bloodstream, the laserlight racing through every muscle. The feel of Sammy's hands up her back, pulling her hips against his as they gyrated in the centre of the dance-floor. His hands sliding down the back of her jeans—

—waltzing up the empty high street, staggering across the bridge, a bend and lift up her front door step, and a frenzied undressing as he pushed her up the stairs, hands grabbing at clothes, pulling up to reveal tantalising skin. He had her naked by the landing, shoving her up against the door of her bedroom, sliding two fingers between her legs and digging. He thrust his face into her neck, whispering. "Yeah, sugar, how's that? You like that?"

Bloody hell, he couldn't find his way if I drew him a diagram. She groped for the door-handle and they fell onto her floor in a tangle of limbs. She pulled off his shirt, ran her hands down his naked torso. God, she needed this—it had been too long since a good honest shag. Ages since the last time she'd felt the collision of bodies, skin on skin, the pleasure pulsing outwards between them. What housewives called *making love.* She unzipped him as she kissed him, yanked him towards and into her.

Then he flipped her on her front. She felt carpet burns up her chest as he shoved his weight on top of her and the

heat on his body - rapidly turning cold - with the back of his hand.

"Oh dear! Here let me help you," Samantha said, snatching a tea-towel from the countertop. She began thrusting the towel vigorously into the stained area.

"Samantha, it's quite alright..."

"I would never have supposed you were a clumsy man, Mr Dashby! Not with those big strong hands. Oh my!"

Samantha's enthusiastic efforts had extended to other areas of his clothing and had become more vigorous. Dashby failed to restrain his tea with the force of the thrusts and he felt another warm, wet explosion, this time on his trousers.

"Goodness me, it looks as if clumsiness is contagious!" she indicated the growing dark patch on his trousers. "You should remove these immediately. I'll fetch some spares from the linen closet upstairs. Wait here, I will return!"

And with that she left, leaving Dashby standing awkwardly in his soiled garments.

From somewhere upstairs a cackle of laughter erupted, followed by short applause. He wondered if he should take the opportunity to make his escape. Samantha was an accommodating girls, that much was clear, but her advances were destined to fail: Dashby had already been put off by the fusty nature of the courtship ritual, one he was doomed to repeat endlessly within the corseting confines of Compton House.

Tea was a temporary refuge. He mourned the loss of his last cup.

"One new message, sir," came a voice from the doorway.

heat of his body on her back. He yanked her hair and kissed her neck as he shoved roughly into her, moaning.

Small, hard and circular.

And that was all she felt, apart from a stabbing pain, and tears welling up. She stared blankly ahead at the edge of her curtains as daylight started to filter past them until he shuddered, and rolled off.

She dragged her body up onto the bed and wrapped herself in her duvet. Sammy lay passed out on the floor. He hadn't even bothered to take his trousers fully off. He lay on his back in the remnants of the warm, wet explosion. A strong desire to stamp on him arose in her.

Daylight slowly oozed across the walls. The room filled with a damp grey light. Bex just lay there, staring across the room.

An hour later, she silently slipped out of the bed, and padded down the stairs, collecting her clothes, listening for the creak of any of her housemates stirring. Nothing, and no-one. Retreating back to bed, she checked her phone—No Messages.

She opened a new message, stared at the blinking cursor, wondered who she could text. The drug he'd given her—that bastard—were starting to leave her system now, her limbs beginning to deaden, her whole body feeling drowsy. She couldn't face sleep though.

So instead, she started typing, haltingly, a message. With no idea of its destination, no intentions of anyone ever reading it, she filled the lines with her thoughts.

When she had finished, she pressed send.

t w o

Im sick of being an object. I like sex trust me
but im sick of just being used. I dont no
who to talk to about this, or if anyone would
understand. I feel like screaming, ripping up
the world, because breaking it apart
with my bare hands is the only way
it'll ever notice. I am SO much more.

Tb x

DASHBY SQUINTED AT the shakily scrawled note the messenger had delivered. The item was initially difficult to decipher, the language oddly hyperbolic and poorly punctuated. At first, he thought the tirade was some sort of furious accusation aimed at him, so infused with rage were the words. But on closer inspection, the pain they carried seemed to lack direction, fuelled more by desperation than purpose. Most perplexingly, he could not recall being familiar with anyone bearing the initials T.B.x.

Dashby headed through from the pantry and out into the main hall. The merry revelry of the manor's

The sound of the alarm was *not* the most pleasant awakening. It hammered around inside Bex's barely-functioning morning-after brain, seeking attention. As did the slam of the front door, the relentless thundering of the bus up to campus, and the din of the thronging students.

Bex found herself—by some unlikely miracle—slumped in the back of a lecture hall, thinking that first-year Philosophy class was the very last place she wanted to be with a hangover and a throbbing comedown. Rick, the grey-haired lecturer who Bex reckoned was a dead ringer guests had reduced to a subdued murmur. He spied the butler, busily sweeping up frozen leaves out in the courtyard at the front of the house. He opened the main door, stepped out into the frosty night air and took a long, ennervating breath.

"Robert," he called to the butler.

"Sir?" said Robert, duly standing to attention and brandishing the broom as if it were a rifle butt.

"This message, when did it arrive?"

"This very evening, I believe, sir. It must have missed the afternoon post. Do you wish to send a reply?"

The question caught him off-guard. He had been so startled by the impassioned vocabulary in the note he hadn't even considered what an appropriate reply ought to be. Not knowing the identity of the sender only added to the uncertainty.

for Einstein, was droning on about his usual crap.

Several forgotten things jumped on her all at once. First: Sammy was still passed out on her floor. She'd totally ignored him when she fumbled out an hour ago. Second: her matching lingerie set was still hanging from the banister rail. Third: she'd sent an embarrassing rambling drunken text message to... God, who?

She snuck out her phone under the table and checked her sent messages. '*I feel like screaming...*'—*what am I, thirteen? I gotta stop this.*

Weirdly, there was a blank space where the name of whoever she'd sent it was. She started to flip through her phonebook, to see if she could find a number.

"Excuse me. Phone." She shoved the phone away under one of her

He examined the heading of the letter again; sure enough, as he had first seen, the address of Compton House was roughly legible alongside a number he did not recognise. An inaccuracy in the date caught his eye: December 3rd 2006? He reread the body of the message, curiosity piqued. Had the sender intended to reach *him* specifically? The humourless prude? The brooding recluse, merely the sum of his parents' success?

No answer presented itself.

Dashby returned to the main hall, his mind a myriad of deliberations. The tone of the message indicated a woman, and an inarticulate one at that. He repeatedly folded and unfolded the note, as if to expose a further clue to the puzzle that gripped him. He wondered aloud: "Who are you?"

legs and tried, completely unconvincingly, to look oblivious. Rick wasn't fooled.

"Kindly switch your phones off in my lectures. Now… where were we? Ah, yes, Rebecca. Could you kindly answer the question: 'who are you?'"

Bex stared blankly at him. Several answers buzzed across her brain. *Pilled-up tart on a comedown. A lost girl. Sum of my parents' failures.*

She managed, "No idea," and shrugged.

Rick blinked glacially at her then spun and waved his cane at the board. "Precisely! Who really can say who they are? Despite this, however, that's precisely the assignment. I want you to think, very hard, for a definition of 'who are you?'"

He ran his finger along the erroneous date and strange number next to the familiar address, and furrowed his brow.

Warm tea and inviting sheets had cast their thrall upon him by the time he had reached his bedchamber. The enigma had exasperated him, and his eyes were heavy with sleep. Slumping onto the four poster bed, he pressed the mysterious epistle to his chest and gave a heavy sigh. Any attempt for further contemplation proved fruitless and he succumbed to fatigue.

He had only begun to drift off when the sound of a note being pushed under the door roused him. Samantha's soft footsteps receded down the corridor outside. Dashby trudged over to the note, and examined it. It read:

A perfect gentleman?

Bex shuffled out the lecture hall with the rest of the dazed early-morning students, spurred by the fantasy of coffee and the warmth of her bed. The route to the bus-stop ran the wild frontier of leaflet-pushers who eagerly thrust club night flyers into her hand whether she opened her fingers to accept or not. She had been told by a lecturer that at least being handed them was a reliable indicator of youth, but for now she'd rather not see neon reminders of Comptons every three steps.

Sammy was long gone by the time she got home. The lingerie on their wooden hanger had been cheerfully pinned to her door by Jake, her housemate, with a post-it reading:

you great big ho ;-)

The question mark was clearly an invitation, as was the receding sound of her footsteps, headed for her bedchamber, but it was not an invitation he found himself inclined to accept. He snuffed out the candle by the bedside and turned his head to face the window. It had begun to snow, and the glistening flakes pirouetted before the glass, sending dancing shadows across the room. The stars were evenly scattered about the blanket of night sky, blinking knowingly at him. He wished, if only for a moment, to borrow their perspective, stare into the eyes of another looking up at them.

Dashby cleared his throat and, staring fixedly into the building blizzard outside, and spoke out his reply to the letter just loud enough for the stars to hear:

She threw the underwear and note in a pile in the corner and collapsed onto her bed. The curtains were drawn, the room comfortingly gloomy. She sank face-first into the bed, arms outstretched like a snow angel. At some point last night she must have lit the fairy-lights that surrounded her bed. They looked down on her like curiously ordered stars. It reminded her of being a kid, when she used to lie on her windowsill, staring up as evening melted into night.

Her laptop beeped as an email popped up in its little blue box in the corner of the screen.

You have received an email from <no sender>.

She clicked it.

It read:

Who are you?

* * *

WHEN DASHBY OPENED his eyes again, the moonbeam had been replaced by a brazen shaft of sunlight that rudely intruded into the bedchamber. He turned himself towards the bedside table and saw it instantly: a new note beside the one from before, though he had heard no-one deliver it. Cautiously, he picked it up and unfolded it.

Bex stared blankly at the three words on the screen. No sender—how weird. She clicked the reply button, and hovered her fingers over the keys. The blank page of the email stared back at her, daring her.

This is ridiculous. I don't even know who I'm writing this to. Then: *Why not?*

She started typing:

I am several things: a girl, a teenager and a legal adult, though that last one is as surprising to me as everyone else. I am the daughter of a plumber who left when I was four, and a beauty therapist. My mother is only fifteen years older than me, and her last boyfriend was younger than me, which if I believed in lazy psychology I'd say probably explains why I just sleep with guys instead of being in a relationship with them. I'm cynical and homesick for a time 'before', but I don't know when that ever was. I can't find any way to connect to my friends here, and all I wish at the moment was that there was someone to just listen to me.

Dashby reread the letter four or five times before remembering to draw any breath. It bore the same strange number and date, and the penmanship matched the first he had received, but if a little more measured, more controlled. The furious tone had been succeeded by a pervading sense of melancholy. Some of the words were alien to him: he pondered the significance of "boyfriend" and "guys". Most striking though, the ending of the letter resonated profoundly with him: As he ruminated on the words, the ink glinted at him as if still wet. *Just listen to me.*

With renewed vitality, Dashby burst from the room and marched off towards his study, clutching the precious document tightly. He snatched the quill from his writing desk

Seconds after hitting the send button, she regretted it. None of the words she'd written seemed to have shaped themselves properly. On the page, it sounded so drearily teenage. *Look at me, I'm so screwed up, love me!* She was almost certain it wasn't what Rick had been looking for by way of an answer. Hers was definitely a life story that would need a bit of re-drafting.

And not only that, but she had sent this tired rant out into the ether where god knows who would read it. She half-expected spam to pop into her email box: "Tired of life? Absent father? Inappropriate mother? Moronic friends? Never worry again with penis extensions from CyniCorp!"

and began to scribe in his best calligraphy:

With that, the email pinged:

Dear T.B.x,

It is my highest hope that you get this letter. Have I previously had the pleasure of your acquaintance? If the answer to that is yes, then you must forgive my lack of recollection. In any case, I profess that your words have become the recent object of my obsession.

Though I know little of who you are, or how you came to write to me, it is my wish that you know this:

I am listening.

Sincerely,

William Dashby

He sealed the letter with a wax stamp and held it in both hands for a few moments. Then he pushed his chair back and stood resolutely, striding out of the study and back to the main hall. He found Robert on his hands and knees, polishing ornaments in the leisure room.

So not only was her email talking to her, it also wrote in full formal letter form and copperplate font. And who the hell was Tbx?

Bex really wasn't in the mood for this. She slammed down the laptop lid and rolled over on her side.

"Robert, do you have a return address for this letter?"

Robert looked up from his labour, and smiled curiously at the article being held towards him.

"Don't worry about that, sir," he said. "You leave that to me."

* * *

THE NEXT MESSAGE came just as quickly, and Dashby risked damaging it in his keenness to open it. His hands trembled as he scanned the words on the page.

Writing the first email seemed to have drained her. No bad thing—that had perhaps been the idea after all. But the last thing she felt like doing now was writing more about herself. Especially to some disembodied person— what was the name at the bottom? William Dashby.

The name struck her as familiar, like she'd read it somewhere before, but she couldn't think why. She reached back for the laptop and brought herself up an internet page.

William Dashby? *Obviously* you must mean Sir William Dashby, of Compton Hall…the one that's a club now? See, I googled your ass! Seriously though, who actually are you? I don't really feel like ranting anymore—all ranted out!—and it's kinda made it all feel a bit pointless. Sorry for you having to read all that, I really should stop drinking!

PS. My name's not Tbx, you must have misread – it's Bex.

Dashby was once again left bamboozled by the message, but it was a feeling he enjoyed: one of pleasant discombobulation. It appeared as though the sender knew of him, though his station was no secret to the townspeople, but "googled your ass" baffled him. He wondered whether his new pen-friend was even native to English shores. In either case, he knew he hadn't misread the sign-off T.B.x.

He grasped his quill.

Closing the lid, she was surprised to find herself anticipating a reply with a degree of excitement, and wishing she'd managed to be just a little wittier.

Imagine if it was the nineteenth century Dashby. She amused herself with elaborate Victorian gent fantasies, mostly involving lakes and wet shirts, novel uses for canes and a prodigious number of top hats.

Beep! Inbox:

Dear Miss Bex

I assumed you might already know who I am, seeing as it was you who initiated our discourse and addressed your message to my residence. Your name is very unusual, I've never before encountered one like it. Are you from an exotic land? I must inform you that I have in my possession no beasts of burden, so it is not my ass that you encountered. Are you certain you have the right person?

Yours sincerely,

William Dashby of Compton House

The response was almost immediate, despite the worsening winter weather.

Victorian it was then! She set about formulating her reply, chewing her nails fretfully.

Actually, my name's Rebecca, but I don't like it. So Bex it is! Sorry, but I actually don't know who you are, I'm not even sure how my message got to you. Still, you seem nice—you're not an axe murderer or anything are you? Promise? My mother warned me against talking to strangers, but sod that—*carpe diem* and all. Tell me about yourself, Mr Dashby. Do you by any chance know a Mr Darcy? :P

Bex xx

Dashby smiled as he read the letters, and placed each carefully inside his bedside drawer of personal effects. Each new one fed his curiosity, and gave him shallow glimpses of a face he had never laid eyes on. Each strange word or misplaced punctuation mark seemed to carry with it a small hint of

She focused on distracting herself, determined not to just sit around waiting. Her heart was beating just a little faster—she felt like a schoolgirl giggling with her friends when the boy they all fancied looked over at her. Which was, as far as she was concerned, ridiculous.

her perfume, a flash of her smile.

Dashby revelled in writing back.

All good intentions, and all that; the beep of her email sent her scrambling up stairs.

Dearest Rebecca,

What a beautiful name. Your mother's advice is sound, but please know that I am not now nor ever will be inclined to indulge in acts of murder. I'm much more likely to enjoy a cup of Earl Grey and a punt on the lake. I take it from the latin reference you're familiar with the works of Horace then? I find it all a bit heavy going, I'm more partial to a bit of Dickens before retiring! How do you like to pass the time? I very much look forward to your next letter.

Yours sincerely,

W. Dashby

On the days between letters, Dashby found himself at his usual sentry post by the window, sipping tea and staring out. He had the lingering hope

Bex found herself - against her better judgement and own good sense - grinning widely.

All the memories of the night before, of Sammy,

that if he stood long enough, he might see the postal carriage arrive out of the white miasma, carrying with it the next precious message. He never quite managed to catch it. Even so, the rules of courting women were made more obsolete with every intimate note that Rebecca sent him.

Soon enough, he stopped finding the more obscure phrases she employed jarring or esoteric. He drank in the sweet sentiment and savoured it, like a fine Darjeeling.

scuttled into the back corners of her mind. She really did feel like she was back in school, fidgeting in front of a messenger screen, learning the rules of talking to boys—that familiar somersault of the stomach every time a new message arrived.

She didn't even stop and think about what she was writing this time. She just let the words pour out of her.

Punting and tea? Rock and roll. I'm more of a dancing and whiskey girl myself. We studied Horace this year in Philosophy. Wasn't a fan. But enough about my uni course, can't have you think I'm boring!

And you know what, Bill... I look forward to your next letter too!

Bex xxxx

P.S. Why do you show up as nothing?

t h r e e

AN UNFAMILIAR SCENE trundled by the window of the carriage to town. Dashby gazed out of it and admired the transforming effect that two week's heavy snowfall could have. During the Christmas period, Dashby had always found it necessary to leave Compton, to fleetingly escape the prison the place had become, his cradle.

The familiar roads sprawled past the windscreen as Bex drove through her old hometown. The last two weeks of term had been winding down to this— the first return home, relinquishing to the pull of a family Christmas.

Here we go, crawling back to the womb.

Everything seemed bigger in town than in the country where the manor lay. A restless energy could be felt throbbing through its heart, as if ready to spill to the edges. The streets were tinged with incandescent light. And yet for all its gaslit splendour, Dashby could not help but find it overwhelming. He shied away from it.

The anticipated cliche stood true: the town did seem smaller, all of the roads shorter. Even her mum's car—a bright yellow Mini— seemed to have faded.

Yet the town did served its purpose as a distraction.

She had deliberated about all of her packing,

It stopped Dashby fixating on the one thing he yearned to see: Rebecca's next message, unfolded in his hands. He hadn't spent a single night at Compton House without the bedside drawer open, its treasured contents strewn over the bedsheets where he slept. For him, the last month had lingered on unbearably, with social gatherings at the mansion becoming less of a faint irritance and more what Bex would describe as 'a total drag'. The laboured procedure of courtship continued: the ladies graciously fawned and curtseyed, and Dashby reciprocated impeccably. It was a routine he could step through with both eyes closed, and so he did. While effortlessly reciting platitudes and performing feats of chivalry, he counted down the long seconds that filled the gaps between his moments alone with the letters. His interludes by the window grew more frequent, and his lookout for the postal delivery became habitual. Occasionally, he took to watching the kettle in the pantry instead, waiting for it to boil.

fussing and worrying for nearly the whole fortnight. In the end, she had thrown a bag of random clothes in the back of the car and decided to live with whatever came out. (That, and the box of email printouts on the passenger seat. Of course.)

The last month for her had seemed to go at speed — faster by half than all of the dreary others.

She counted time in gaps between checking her email, and found herself unconciously doodling rough cartoons of a

The carriage slowed to a halt and Dashby assembled his town-coat, pocket hat and walking stick. He gave a small nod to Robert holding the door open as he stepped out of the carriage and onto the cobbled street. While he searched his pockets for gloves, his hand brushed paper. One of the few letters from Bex he always carried with him. Something had been made indecipherable at the bottom of the page. One day he would ask her what it was.

The market was a hive of activity. "Apples!" "Pies!" "Meat!" "Here!" It seemed extraneous syllables had no place in the centre of town.

Victorian gentleman— frock coat, top hat, cane —in the margins of her notes. One time, she thought he winked up at her. At one insufferable juncture she'd caught herself writing I ♥ **Dashby** on the bottom of her Aristotle paper, then quickly scrubbed it out in embarassment.

Her mother launched herself at her like a pitbull, shrieking before Bex was across the front porch.

"Rebeccccca! Daaaaarling! It's so good to see you. You're looking a bit... pudgy. You'd best have been eating properly at that university, young lady."

"Yes, mum." Bex suspected that most of her mother's speech was informed by daytime TV, and that she didn't

Dashby browsed the food stalls apathetically. He thought of the corsetted ladies who attended banquets at Compton only to peck at the food like sparrows. Unnaturally gaunt seem to be a universal aspiration.

Dashby allowed himself to be immersed in his bustling surroundings, and attempted to occupy himself in any way possible. He perused the trinket stores, milliners, and even stopped briefly in a busy tavern. He kept a purposeful stride, marching back and forth along the icy cobbles, inviting diversion at every turn. But inevitably, his mind turned to his pocket, to the letter within, and to Miss Bex.

mean a great deal of it. She'd been watching diet programs for as long as Bex could remember. 'Unnaturally gaunt' was a compliment in her book.

As befitting such a long-awaited return to the old homestead, Bex retired to the sofa, and nested there all afternoon, watching TV. Her mum rushed back and forth unleashing an innocuous wave of hometown babble that intermittently pierced the turned-down sussurus of canned laughter. Bex let her mind drift to Mr Dashby.

What was

she doing	he doing
now, he	now, she
wondered.	wondered.
He pictured	She pictured

her riding cars or planes, or any other manner of odd contraption she had described, perhaps to the 'supermarket': his mind boggled at the sheer enormity implied.

He started to question what he could possibly offer a woman like Bex. A caring, reliable man: was that really what she desired? He let his hopes rise before letting them go again.

All he had left to hold on to were the words. Her strange and beautiful words. He clutched the note in his pocket ever more tightly.

He imagined her before him. He pictured them both in the dappled shade of some romantic idyll, her sighing as he put his arms around her. And he kept them there.

him out hunting, shooting pheasants or grouse in the grounds of his country manor.

"So, have you found yourself a man yet?"

"Mum..."

"What? It's about time you found a caring, reliable man. Your track record is terrible. First you let them in your knickers, then you let them go!"

"Mum!"

"I'm only saying! What do you think of these jeans, by the way. Are they too tight?"

"Not for a hooker."

"Ideal."

Her mother turned this way and that, and wiggled.

Bex closed her eyes and sighed. She'd been here an

Evening came and, having terminated his excursion, Dashby rode back to Compton House. The manor loomed on the horizon as the carriage approached, and Dashby felt a curious dread come upon him, a feeling that he had never really left it.

He soon found himself wandering the corridors, running his fingers along the oak panelling of the walls. Everything in its place, as Robert had arranged, and absolutely nothing was right. He staggered up the stairway, collapsed into the bedchamber and yanked open the drawer. He didn't want to be here. This place was no longer his home. He wanted to be wherever she was.

afternoon and already time was crawling.

"I'm just going out for a bit, will you be okay on your own?"

"Fully functional adult here, remember."

"Of course you are, darling."

In her mother's absence, Bex slouched around the house. Everything felt oddly off-kilter, like the house was a painstaking recreation of itself, for a film or a museum, perfectly accurate but not quite...true. Looking at the front door mat, brashly announcing "Welcome Home", it clicked. That was the difference—it wasn't home anymore. It was just a house.

He pulled one of the letters from the drawer. It spoke of the first time her mother had taken her to horse-riding lessons, at nine years old. The horse had reared up, kicking its feet and she had gotten scared. He'd told her that there was no need to be scared of horses, and that there were horses in the field next to the manor in summer, and how he would take her to watch them run.

As he looked down at the letter, he felt the strange feeling that she was looking back

One of the messages from Dashby crossed her mind. He'd told her how the only good memory of his father was cloud-spotting with him in his infancy, conjuring shapes out of the sky. And then she'd told him—for the second time—how she used to lie on the kitchen steps and watch the clouds as a child. It was a very cold day for it, but nevertheless she lay down on the f r e e z i n g concrete and stared up.

He closed his eyes and pressed the letter first to his lips and then to his chest, taking scarce notice of the fresh flakes of snow tapping at the window. It was as if they were asking to come in, or asking him to come out.

*

*

HE THOUGHT HE could make out something in the great white blank before him. He reached out both his arms.

A few solitary flakes of snow drifted down from the watercolour skies and kissed her on the cheek.

*

*

She awoke. Out of the stark greyness, a revelation came. All she wanted right now was to see him, the words made flesh. She longed for him to wrap his arms around her, enfolding her.

Nothing could be heard in the blizzard's embrace, save for three words sent skywards.

*

*

I love you.

four

"Hello Bex."

A smile.

"Hello William."

"You're a lot taller than I imagined."

"Is that a good thing? The heels add a lot."

"You look beautiful."

A blush.

"Is this just a dream?"

"Hasn't it always been?"

"I wish I was with you."

"And I too."

"And then I don't want it to end."

"There is a way."

"Tell me."

"There is a small wood near Compton House, with a willow tree in the centre. Go there at 3 o'clock on the 31st December. That's where I'll be."

"But there are centuries between us."

A final smile.

"And no time at all."

"Wait for me."

Snow had begun to settle upon the floor of the copse by the time Bex had arrived, breathless. She was clutching the stack of Dashby's e-mails between her frost-rimed gloves, a red ribbon tied round the bundle. The wind was picking up; it rasped through the trees and kept blowing the hood of her jacket off her head.

The wood was small and she reached the clearing where the willow tree stood easily. There was no one in sight. She wiped the snowflakes from the screen of her phone to check the time, before scanning the clearing again. Was she too late?

It was then that she noticed it.

On a small spot on the willow where no snow had

gathered, there was a tiny carving. She stepped forward to get a better look. The little carving was a stick figure of a girl with one hand on her hip. The other held the hand of a taller figure, dressed in a top hat and a cane.

Cut underneath, the words:

I WILL WAIT FOR YOU ALWAYS

He had been here. She stood for a while tracing the carving with her fingers, and smiled.

On the walk back she stopped at the edge of the wood and undid the ribbon binding the messages. They took flight in the wind, circling skywards. Silently, ecstatically, Dashby's words danced a waltz in the air, until they settled somewhere, like confetti, on the banks of renewing snow.

Inside a place   Untouched by time

Two books are sitting   side by side

the gap between   becoming small

Until there is no gap at all

high on a shelf

where hearts sing

in a room

forever

(Whispering)